Bear's Birthday
El cumpleaños de Oso

Stella Blackstone
Debbie Harter

Bear has blown up ten big balloons.
His party guests will be here soon!

10

Oso ha inflado diez globos grandes.
¡Sus invitados a la fiesta están por llegar!

**Bear opens the door to welcome his friends.
He's hoping his day of fun never ends.**

9

Oso abre la puerta para recibir a sus amigos.
Espera que este día divertido no termine nunca.

**The first game they play is hide-and-seek.
Where is Bear? Can you see his feet?**

8

Primero juegan al escondite.
¿Dónde está Oso? ¿Puedes ver sus pies?

Next they all play musical chairs.
There's not enough room for so many bears.

7

Justo después juegan a las sillas.
No hay lugar para tantos osos.

The group hunts for treasure among the trees.
Bear crouches down: guess what he sees!

6

El grupo busca tesoros entre los árboles.
Oso se agacha: ¡adivina qué ve!

**Bear unwraps the treasure and looks inside.
He has a wonderful birthday surprise!**

Oso abre el tesoro y mira adentro.
¡Es un maravilloso regalo de cumpleaños!

It's full of delicious jam and honey:
Raspberry, strawberry, apricot, cherry.

4

Está lleno de deliciosa mermelada y miel:
de frambuesa, fresa, albaricoque, cereza.

**The table is covered with tasty treats.
It's time for Bear's big birthday feast!**

La mesa está cubierta con ricas golosinas.
¡Es el momento del gran festín de Oso!

Bear blows out his candles with one big puff.
When he slices his cake, there's just enough.

2

Oso apaga las velas con un gran soplido.
Cuando corta el pastel, alcanza para todos.

"Goodbye, Bear, and thank you," his visitors say.
"We've all had lots of fun today!"

—Adiós, Oso, y gracias —dicen sus invitados.
—¡Nos hemos divertido mucho hoy!

Counting Balloons

Who is making the balloons disappear?
Can you help Bear count down from 10 to 1?

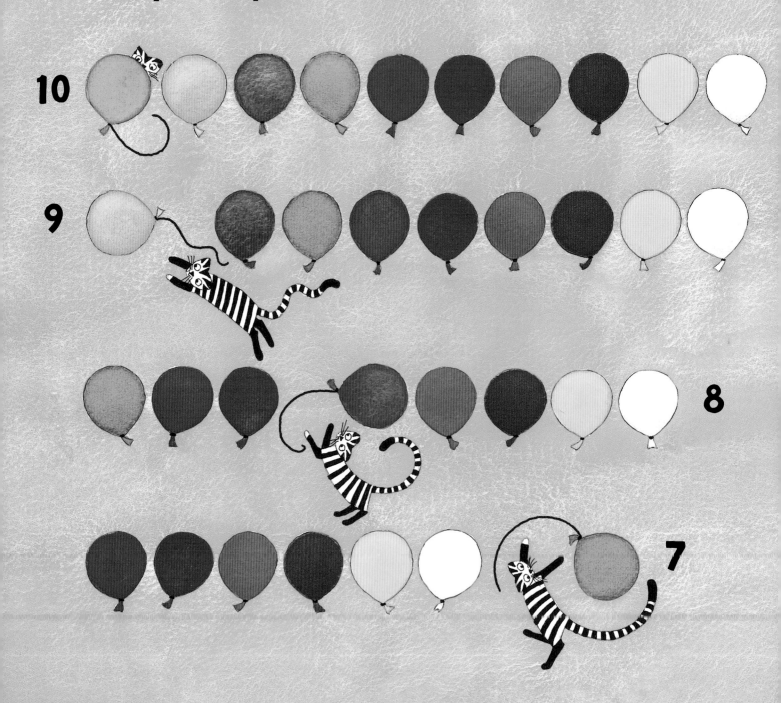

Contar globos

¿Quién hace desaparecer los globos?
¿Puedes ayudar a Oso a contar del 10 al 1?

Vocabulary / Vocabulario

one – uno
two – dos
three – tres
four – cuatro
five – cinco
six – seis
seven – siete
eight – ocho
nine – nueve
ten – diez

Barefoot Books   Barefoot Books
294 Banbury Road   2067 Massachusetts Ave
Oxford, OX2 7ED   Cambridge, MA 02140

Text copyright © 2011 by Stella Blackstone
Illustrations copyright © 2011 by Debbie Harter
The moral rights of Stella Blackstone and Debbie Harter have been asserted

First published in Great Britain by Barefoot Books, Ltd
and in the United States of America by Barefoot Books, Inc in 2011
This bilingual Spanish edition first published in 2013

Graphic design by Judy Linard, London and Louise Millar, London
Reproduction by B & P International, Hong Kong
Printed in China on 100% acid-free paper
This book was typeset in Futura and Slappy
The illustrations were prepared in paint, pen and ink, and crayon

ISBN 978-1-84686-943-3

British Cataloguing-in-Publication Data:
a catalogue record for this book is available from the British Library

Library of Congress Cataloging-in-Publication Data
is available upon request

Translated by María Pérez

1 3 5 7 9 8 6 4 2